SONGS
A THRACIAN
TAUGHT ME

To David Storey & Jonathan Barker
friends and fellow travellers
and to
Veronica Ann
who has just begun the journey

By the same author

Walking Without Moving (Turret Books, 1967)
The Lair (Rapp & Whiting, 1968)
Footsteps On Snow (Agenda Editions, 1972)
The Curving Shore (Agenda Editions, 1975)
Alexandros: translation of selected poems by Vera Lungu (Agenda Editions, 1975)

Acknowledgements

Agenda, Akzente, Gallery, Unicorn Press, Boston University Journal, New Statesman

This book has been published with financial assistance from the Arts Council of Great Britain

SONGS A THRACIAN TAUGHT ME

Anne Beresford

MARION BOYARS
LONDON · BOSTON

First published in Great Britain and the United States in 1980
by Marion Boyars Publishers Ltd.
18 Brewer Street, London W1R 4AS
and Marion Boyars Publishers Inc.
99 Main Street, Salem,
New Hampshire 03079

Australian distribution by Thomas C. Lothian
4-12 Tattersalls Lane, Melbourne, Victoria 3000.

British Library Cataloguing in Publication Data
Beresford, Anne
Songs a Thracian taught me.
I. Title
821'.9'14 PR6052.E56S/ 80-40536

Library of Congress Catalog Card Number: 80-40536

ISBN 0 7145 2724 6 cased edition
ISBN 0 7145 2725 4 paper edition

Printed in Great Britain by
Redwood Burn Limited
Trowbridge & Esher

CONTENTS

DIPLOMA

Virgo without a rising sign
The day – Monday
The month – September
The time – forgotten
It rained just before breakfast
And the man, no great hero,
loved his wife, promising her things
which in the end
amounted to misunderstandings

Beyond the wood,
said grandmother,
is a road
rocky, deserted
nothing grows there
a few birds skim
never lingering
Take care
to avoid it

The world,
said grandfather
is an exciting place
I've travelled everywhere
in Russia the snow
would have covered you

Men, said mother, are liars
Women, said father, never tell the truth

The Amazon is in South America,
said teacher,
yellow and blue make green
Napoleon came from Corsica
You, child, are an imbecile

Don't cry
don't speak to me like that
don't be naughty
don't fidget
Watch the birdie,
said grandfather
And took a photograph

INTERROGATION

The methods hardly vary
only the questions you ask yourself
until you break
not on Friday
not even Saturday
but much later
when it is too late to step back
your whispers will formulate
the answers

THE COURTSHIP

I am curiously stirred
by the landscape
as I wait lazily for
my lover
lazily in the hot sun

no hurry
life goes on
time to admire
my long thin arms
they blend with
the long thin grass
their frailty is deceptive
my lover will not be the first
to know their strength

strange to consider
how small he always is
true, he moves gracefully
but never quick enough

when he is joined to me
too absorbed to notice
my knife-like grip
I will eat him inch by inch
I'll not need another meal
for many hours

afterwards I will sit quietly
under the exotic leaves
raising my arms again
as if praying

DAY DUTY

The cuckoo, doctor, is my alarm clock in the summer.
Without moving from the bed, at his first call,
I see the garden quivering expectantly,
freshly damp – a world renewed.
I lie amazed at such perfection.

The cat, doctor, is the bell for breakfast,
ever insistent, her amber eyes fixed on mine
her claws sharpened to receive the contents of a tin.
And all the time the birds chattering;
I move slowly, surely, gathering momentum to face
the day.

Such an efficient system.
The bees, doctor, are my example.
Monotonous buzzing, bumbling in and out the
startling colours.
The moorhen's eggs have hatched and
the swallows glide from the boiler house.
It all runs according to the plan.

Yes, doctor, give me your draught
of forget-me-nots and orange flower
the patients in my care too sane, too logical.
I need the long, cool drink which leaves my mind in
heaven
My body in a state of fine imbalance.

NIGHT DUTY

The scud has crossed the heath
enveloping everything in clammy breath.
I can just make out the shape of a horse on the roof
and a mammoth grazing on the lawn.
The time between day and night
last chirrupings, daisies curled, a pheasant's
squawk from somewhere in the field.
Lights on in the village.
Reporting for duty in the T. V. room, doctor.

Each piece of furniture is alone
isolated where the floorboards creak without being
trodden on.
Incantations are useless. Let the blood be,
it flows like water from the gutter.
Photographs on a screen.
Shadows on a screen.
The moon comes up behind the willow tree.
On watch. Bemused. Stunned.

. . . TO THOSE WHO SLEEP IN DUST

And the sun
sets peacefully
behind the pine trees
the sky growing deep
deeper
till it has swallowed the last
tip of grass

And we close our eyes
trusting
that we shall be able to open them
we walk trustingly
into the arms of our executioners
we walk lightly
on the blood spattered pavements
we obey the commands of others
who also trust others
who trust they are right
and the earth
trembles, pales

And the sun shines
how it shines, warms,
transforms the dust
into shimmering sparks
the smoke into blue shreds of clouds
pushes its soft fingers
through the cold flesh
to touch the marrow of cold bones

NON HAPPENING

Neither to blame.
A momentary loss of control
on both sides.
The encounter could almost be called
radiant, for one of them.
Left – an afternoon of sunshine,
a few hours of discussion
and a handprint
burning into her flesh.

THE GREAT MAN IS DEAD . . .

for Anna Dostoievsky

When he lay dying he worried
about the fate of his family:
'What am I leaving you with, my dearest?
My poor girl, how will you live?'
As always his wife soothed him.
He died peacefully.

She survived.
Long enough to bring up his children,
publish his collected works,
found a school in his name,

compile a bibliography, sort letters, papers,
and see them placed in a new museum.
She wrote and re-wrote her story of their marriage.
A deathly survival. It kept her sane.

At the funeral, someone remembered seeing her –
draped in black, heavily veiled,
befitting a modest widow. Two children at her side.
A touching picture.

All the devotion, self sacrifice, love
ended years later, in a cold room.
She died painfully.
Was he with her, in spirit, to comfort
her last hours?
There was no-one else.
She was his wife. Nothing more.
Nothing less.

THE CAPTIVE

based on a Russian Folk Tale

Back and forth
along the shore
of this deserted beach
disconsolate
her dress wet round the hem
billowing in the wind
like her hair
tangled
salt sprayed.
This, the one place
where she can walk freely
never free of the rocky house
perched so crazily on the cliff side
never free of the love
which led to this prison.
'Inviolable,' he'd say, laughing,
'my name is Deathless.'
She kicked against the stones
where did he keep his death?
In a kernel
in a nut
in a worm
on a shrub
in a garden
inaccessible?

'Tell me, my dear,
your secret.
The bones of my pursuers

lie dry and clean
on the road to this fortress.
But I have talked with
the winds and the sea
my strength is failing.
I dream of your hands smoothing my hair
I dream of your voice soothing my fears.
In the daylight
I hear your laughter echoing
in the high chimneys
and I see my own reflection
in the polished wood of the table.'

NARCISSUS

He saw a new aspect of himself
transfigured for a moment
by his brilliant eyes

Becoming whole
he heard his sorrowful echo
echo:
I love you
you

THE COLLECTOR

for Peter Kaplan

Grey the stone
the sky
your basket dragging
your steps
back from the grocer
the butcher
the candlestick maker
under the clouds
rain
sometime sun

at the street corner
scatter the lightfooted
the tender, all
those whose turn has come
to ride upon the winds
from North or South
East or West

Grey your face
grey your clothes
lonely
walking through the front door
of your grey life
little island
isolated
in the bay
of your window

is this it, then?
a kind of discarding
skin of a snake
shed for collectors
to place on the shelf
gathering dust?

Living is a grey matter
in the mind

The children are playing
catch me if you can Mr. Wolf
but supper time is a long way off
They are searching
among stained shadows
mud splattered

They sing an old song
of wild birds and snake calls
and the word's flutter of scarlet

Their front doors are closing
stone upon stone
blocks the bay of the window

The collector has turned
to dust on the shelf

MODERN FAIRY TALE

Once, not long ago,
a princess lived in a tower
at Factory Junction.
Locked up by a kind of Black Magic.

When she looked out of the window
she could see the railway lines
the gas works and Battersea Power Station.

Her prince came to visit her
as all princes have always done
at night.
He didn't have to climb her hair
she went whirling down from the eighteenth floor
in a lift.

Horses, known to them both from T.V.
were not practical.
They used a motor bike.

She never danced her shoes to pieces
he never found a dog in a walnut shell
they never knew if they were in love
but as they tore through Battersea
he would think, vaguely, of taking her away
somewhere.

Neither of them realized
that escape was impossible,

and when they sat together in the Wimpy Bar
they talked of living in another tower
on the other side of the river.

There is no end to this story.

IN DEFENCE OF LA BELLE DAME SANS MERCI

She has searched so long
she's even begun to wonder what it is she
searches for,
illusions everywhere she turns.

All those knights in shining armour
pale and dying for want of her
are no more true than their loving protestations.
Their milkwhite steeds just cars
in which she's driven back and forth
admiring different aspects of London life.
Goddess, Nymph, a Faery's Child – mere names.
Her elfin grot a flat with views of other flats,
her children spread around the world.
And when she weeps: 'I love you true'
she, too, means it for a while.

Dust caked on the broken pavements
geraniums growing in grimy windows
someone said: 'I hope you'll be happy'
as he slammed the door. And another said:
'What makes you think because I'm young
I have more hope than you?'

Deserted under a railway arch she dreams of
cancerous growths, deformities, tramping feet
and wailing voices.

Why blame her for her dancing foot
her flowing hair, wild eyes?
She roams, listless, by withered sedge and lake
afraid that the end of disillusion
is only another lie.

SEQUEL TO SOME FAIRY TALES

They were happy.
They were happy.
He carried her away to his castle.

From a distance
in the warm summer night
set among trees and daisy covered fields
it did resemble fairyland.
Not a delicate structure
but moated, built with massive walls and towers,
where, after the second winter,
she shivered and declined.
He had troubles, too.
The land, it seemed, belonged to someone else.
His father had omitted to tell him of the mortgage.
Besides he was oversensitive,
the harsh life, overseeing of criminals
tortures, executions, did not agree with him.
He became morose. Then manic.
At times taking to the woods
he'd howl like an animal in pain.

Who speaks now?
It is I, Marie. Wife of my lord.
Unhappy wife. I looked into the dark
and found no comfort there.
Secret.
Secret is my soul
the walls hold death.
He came quiet and terrible.
All fairy tales finished.

The castle fell to ruins.
Still crumbles.
On warm summer nights,
calm nights
he whirls out of the stillness
tearing at the walls
howling her name –
leaving an equal stillness in his wake.

ORPHEUS ARRIVES IN A NEW WORLD

In order to enter the temple
it is necessary to lift aside the second veil.
It would be easier, Orpheus thought, in another
  country.
Here, all things flourished
whether he sang or no.
The rivers were broader and longer
the trees were taller, mosquitos fiercer
and even the crows spoke a different language.

He put his lyre in a locker at the bus station
and walked into town.
He peered in the wide cracks of paving stones
examining the usual amounts of dirt encrusted there.
He gazed in the windows of broken down houses
admired decrepit elegance, imagining days gone by –
imagining ladies, particularly ladies, with parasols,
lace hankies clutched in little hands,
gleaming teeth, gleaming hair under beribboned
  bonnets.

He loved them all.
Blew kisses through the torn curtains.

An old man sheltering in a porch,
a bottle to his lips, nuzzling with soft gulps,
observed Orpheus as he smiled and bowed
blowing kisses to an unseen audience.
The old tramp laughed and spat:

'Why don't you sing, Orpheus?
This is Hell.'

In order to enter the temple
it is also necessary to pass between the pillars.
Orpheus, hands in pockets striding through dead leaves.
Orpheus, uninspired, stalking through
browns and yellows, taking note
of sounds, colours, sights and smells.
Scowling, his voice tuneless.

He found Eurydice in the kitchen.
His goddess, sitting between the pillars
of sink and gas stove.
'I am the great law,' said Orpheus.
And the woman turned her face to look at him.

PANDORA'S CHILD

for Helen and Franklin Reeve

Again.
Two steps down to the kitchen
through the garden door.
Again someone shouting
somewhere in the hollows of the house.
A child is wandering up and down
in and out.
Not playing –
waiting.
There's no light here
the brown paint chipped.
Strangers pass on the stairs
complaining of the noise.

This child has watched the migrating birds
marvelled at the autumn sun
paddled in icy lakes.
She has picked the last sweet grapes
from a friend's vine in an alien land.
She had hope.
And night after night she returns
to wait on the two dark steps.
And night after night the shouting.
Wet salt on her lips
again.

ECHO OF CONSCIENCE

'These children put us to shame, whilst we
slumber, they set forth gaily,'
Pope Innocent III on the children's crusade.

Dust flew up in clouds
and the clouds over their heads
butterflies
shimmering in hysterical song.

A knot of poverty in the pit of the stomach
they set out for the kingdom of God.
It was the best thing that had happened
to some of them –
leaving the villages
and the knots of parental obedience
which left scars on protruding bones.

At first there was bread, even wine,
prayers, praise and much curiosity
– especially in the soft, supple bodies.
The last chaste knot to be tied or untied.

Naked love would conquer the infidel
since the sword could not.
And the infidel were butterflies
gaudy, exotic. And they were animals
tamed, gentle, miraculously following
the children. Full of trust in their faithfulness.

Many children were thrown into brothels
or sold into slavery.
Some returned later
faith washed off in blood.

And they needed the miracles, the butterflies
to snatch their souls from the bitterness.
Most of them died.

UNHOLY GIVING

based on a spell: How to understand
what the birds are saying

Split leaves
and rotting fungus underfoot
the dogs sniffed out the prey

For you alone
I cooked and such a heart
which cost long nights
I ate
and later heard the pheasant
speak clearly to the sparrow

Dear love, my first kiss was to give you pleasure
For you alone I broke the Fast
If I kiss you twice,
like Eve, I want to share
the unacceptable

LEISTON ABBEY

Through the refectory,
open to the setting sun,
the grass wet, muddy in places
near the chiselled flint,
they passed. Soundlessly,
heads covered, hands concealed,
hugging the walls, to pray
in the Lady Chapel – which remains
intact but locked.
In the uneasy peace of old stones
is a carved rabbit, ears portrayed
by streaks of white, the back smooth
beautifully rounded, shoots of grass
growing over the folded paws.
There are the two of us and stillness.
The stone moves gently
as though a heart were beating quickly.

And bending down I see that the stone
is alive and suffering.
This is its sanctuary.
Nothing makes sense
with the heavy clouds spitting rain
onto the rabbit, its eyes obliterated
by the large swellings of diseased flesh.

THE VISITOR

based round a spell on how to conjure
three people in your room when lonely

Three people came
you stayed
Love would be shameless
if disintegration were not final

When you have eaten the bread,
drunk the water,
simple things
asked for simply
come near me and
I will study the lines
of your face
the shape of your finger nails

nothing more

I will juggle
with swallows
for you
with colours of geraniums
with sea spray
of a minute universe
in the hours of Mercury
in the minutes of June

No law against
your voice
in the hour of Saturn
in the minutes of January
and the longing for you
undiminished
cherished
now I am invisible

Through this window pane
the pear tree
point in sudden space
the alien days
gnarled and blossoming

nameless your presence
in this white washed room
solitary this bed

CANDLEMAS

Candles.
Stone pillars waver and glow
with tiny flames.

This is the time for recollection,
for sowing of seeds
veneration of virgins
a coming of day
a looking forward

In what do we believe?
I find no answer.
For what do we pray?
Metanoia?

We are part
of a skilful tapestry
reflecting the moving year.

GOSSIP

Snow.
Thick snow.
A partridge spied on by a pheasant
searches for food.
The pheasant is closely observed
by the farmer's boy –
he has a gun.
Unknown to him the secret police
are very interested in his movements.
The villagers, naturally curious,
fish for red herrings
in the frozen pond.

SEPTEMBER FABLE

The soldiers were tired.
Coming out from the city
in the crazy heat
to look for a man.

And there was this gardener
watering his strawberries

tending his carrots
bringing his grapes
to the table, his wine.
Sharing his supper.

He told them:
'Tomorrow. Always put off
till tomorrow what could
be done today. Eat now,
be merry, there's plenty of time
for a killing. Tomorrow
I'll show you your man.'

Come morning he stands
with dew on his feet
by a grave dug as carefully
as his asparagus bed.
'Bury me here alongside
my carrots and strawberries.
I am your man.'

The soldiers are sad.
Coming back from the village
blood on their minds
and this gardener
dead in the heat of midday.

BIRD WATCHER

Having lost his footing at an early age
he was stranded in the branches of a city.
He watched the words he could not communicate
fly away in cloud formation.

Separated from himself
he stared at space. Scorning machines.
He longed to part the banks of cloud drift
to rise and fall in shafts of air.
As his bones became heavier
so the desire to fly became greater.

After years of practice, he found
that by walking slowly, his feet
lifted him a short distance from the ground
continuing their walking movement until he was air-
borne.

Cautious, he never attempted this unless
in the right frame of mind.

As he became more experienced
he found it easy to lie in the air horizontally.
Wiser, he no longer tried to fly after the unobtainable.
Disentangling himself from his leafless embrace
he is flying into the silence where
he contains his body.

FARMER'S FANTASY

'It were from a black toad,
with a star on its back
found under an owd felled log,'
his grandfather whispering before he died,
thrusting it into his hand.

And it worked.
Horses obeyed him,
the cow's milk was richer,
crops never failed,
no warts in the family.
Power at his finger tips.
Nothing deceived him.

The tiny thing in his pocket
little black bone
smooth, polished, a fearful inheritance.

If the snow could blanket his thoughts
gently freeze his brain,
cover the furniture that walked in the night
that stood by his bed
in response to his dreams.

Nowhere was safe.
Still he fingered the bane in his pocket,
afraid to think.
Afraid to let go.

'When the snow melts
when the mist rises
when summer comes
when harvest's done
at the next pheasant's call
or the first thunder storm
Then. Then I'll bury it.'

But he couldn't stop thinking.

'I must fetch me a spade from the barn,'
as he left the house,
the spade coming to meet him
you could almost say walking.

LETTER TO CHRISTOPHER

Greetings from the land of make-believe!
Raise your glass
let's drink to life!
It will surprise everyone.

Afternoon of another day
we walk through gates, through fields
the sky rising and dipping
calling: Look! No clouds!
Today – wind, rain.
Leaves tumble bright colours
the swallows gone
mulberries over.
Do you understand the man alone
boxing, whispering insults to his shadow?
The man alone, running
beating time
while two women holding peacock feathers
stare at each other?
Learning has just slipped past –
did you see?
My hands fill with air, fingers swell like sausages,
my head with dried twigs.
What you said was evil is only life
– but treat it with care
watch out for the sting in its tail.

How the rain beats down on the garden chairs.

What matters now is the revolving
of the word-wheel.
Cocooned, marooned in pockets of sun and mist
we live our future in our palms
and float bodiless in night
becoming the words we thought.
Friend, dear friend, did you know
that the wide open spaces
are the gaps in God's mouth?

WHEN YOU COME INTO YOUR COUNTRY

To come out of
be released from
covers a new time

precariously
listening for your approach
I am breathless after
the first few steps

Tree felled
wood splinters
true
A true splinter?

Breathless
absurd
with a splinter on my back
and the borrowed crown
listening, expecting you hourly

The birds have a new time
in the changing moon
The cows on the hill top
are
warriors not animals
and your country is rolling distant

The tree inside me
splinters when I fall
often
with love divorced from love

Remember
let the burning be brief
not in vain
healing
not consuming
when you
come into
your kingdom

FEBRUARY 14th

The sea
swallows the pebbles, throws them up
Afternoon passes
Sun intermittent

To want nothing
to be content with nothing
Needs grow not lessen
Meaning vanishes from time to time
Acts of kindness may be suspect

Heart beat
bird cry
mist
brooding marsh

Railings growing out of the mind
lapped by mist
revealing a spire
and the sea another drumming

Words of love in a foreign language
sea
mist
to send messages through
to penetrate
heaviness

Mind encroaching on
fields
lapped by waves
evening comes with snow

Light in a window
The room glowing in the trees
where the lamps hang in winter air

Returning
through obsequious mist
giving back
And how should it be otherwise?

Only without need is love
Age old gestures of tenderness
and the words of love again and again
carried on the wind

Nothingness is impossible

Illumined
justified
to walk in filled space
enfolded, separate

Not to give
give back
receive

And I have come
hurried, distracted
having done nothing without difficulty

Touching the floor
mute
unable to comprehend the light

THE FIRST SONG OF ALMUT

The unfolding of the earth
the ploughing

sea birds in brown
rising and falling

stretches on towards
heath, heather, broom

finally sea
battering sandy cliffs

Long dreamt of snowdrops
to be sung

by the gentler winds

and it is full turning again
never varying
neither shadow of turning

stiff limbs relax
in the sun's warming

Walking to villages
sounding strangely
contemplation of future
of now
and the bud's bursting

I speak for the women

moods uncertain and restless rain
doubly I live
waiting
a condition of living

And I walk, tired, in the changeable winds
cold, sometimes, singing, singing
for a love to be lightly held

Old woman, I said,
where is your wisdom?

She spread her hands
'In the bones, my love,
in the toughened skin
my hands have touched and
tended all things

In the groaning breath –
do you come near to hear it,
time was when my lungs
filled the moors with laughing –
but in my black skirt and bent back
you'll find no solutions

No, go your way
and I'll go mine

the old one in her days
will not hesitate to ask the babe
about the place of life
it's the years have wings'

Moving always more slowly
on two sticks
she goes before me to sleep abroad

The snow flickers on newly built nests

THE SECOND SONG OF ALMUT

The black dog lopes by my side.
He has taken to following me,
and we find fossils and shells
up here on the wooded heath
where adders bask when there's sun.

Neighbours are afraid of the dog –
not an animal, they say, half human.
Has been seen for nigh on a hundred years,
a devil's pet, they say, be on guard –
a boy was lured into the sea
by a wild, dark man who barked
and yelped as he dragged him down.

Well, dog or no dog
when the mist is over the dead grass
and the owl cries from the willow tree
when the gaunt giants, standing sentry
to the farm, wink as I pass
I pat the rough coat and feel comforted.

The women weave closer
their colours immediate.
Not to mind
the cooking, cleaning
the chatter, nagging,
the scoldings of husband, of children,
which sums up the being of women.

What is happening?
Where are the promises?
The east wind slashes your cheeks
mighty warrior cleaving your skulls
leaving no bruises or blood.
Yet you bleed to death.
How many times will you turn in your grave?

The sea claims the land
fierce is the long fading
bitter the waves

When the bones scream
under the power
colours darken
skies darken

There are men who have power
who control others with a look, a gesture.

The tree of knowledge just out of reach
black wings carry their words on the swell of waves

Time is infirmity

Turn aside, let the air heal
I look towards nothing for a second sight

ELUSIVE LOVE POEM

Master of disguises
you appear in the most unexpected places
– platforms of railway stations
deep footprints in snow drifts
on an icy wind from the east
or at polite dinner parties when
conversation is tiring.
Now, once again, you are near
as I sit in a dirty train
which carries me out of a past I'm unwilling to leave
leading me where I would not go.

Travelling since first light
from North to South
exchanging pleasantries en route
with a travelling juggler and
a musician from Rome.
All passengers pale and anxious.
The effects of a hard winter?
Industrial turmoil?
We are sceptical pilgrims
knowing well that the world has not
promised anything to anybody.

Your hand presses my heart –
the falcon does not struggle when caught.
Your words are always with me.
One day I will sing unrestricted.

BOUNDARIES

Your hand
palm upwards
the untranslatable mist –
I cannot touch you
but I walk towards you
blow you aside
lift you lovingly
through unopened windows

You know how nothing matters but the stones
solitary, circling
and the moment which never passes

It always comes back to this –
after the falling into darkness –
this sun on the grass circle
and a wish for silence

TRUTH UNVEILED

The spring of Time
has dried up
and in the middle of the circle
is a speck of dust

SONGS A THRACIAN TAUGHT ME

The Thracians lamented birth because of the hard life which awaited the newly born. They rejoiced at death and believed they could communicate with the gods. Every five years they chose by lot one among them to send as emissary to Zaimoxis to tell him of their needs. They sent the messenger thus: several soldiers seized him by the arms and legs, several other soldiers stood with spears upright, the messenger was rocked in the air and cast upon the spears. If he died the god was favourable to them. If he lived the messenger was considered an evil man and another messenger was chosen.

They played a game akin to Russian roulette: a warrior stood on a stone with his head through a hangman's noose, holding in his hand his sword. The stone would be kicked away and the game was to cut the rope before it tightened round his neck. Sometimes he was not quick enough and died. The onlookers thought this extremely amusing.

BIRTH

Put on the mask
the lips perfect
the eyes hollow

This is the hard time
And the metal must be beaten
into a shape which weeps

COMMUNICATION

To memorize
words
to be sent
by messenger
to a place
no messenger living
could be sent

To dispatch
a messenger
on spears –
skillfully welded –
held high
for the messenger
to float down on
onwards to another city

To tell the departed
the words
memorized
to describe how
painful
the struggle
to place the feet
on the path
of the living

LOVE SONG OF THE THRACIAN HORSEMAN

I will throw you
only the chicken breast
and the largest crusts
from the whitest bread

You shall drink the best
wine from my cup
your lips on
the imprint of mine

I will give you
seventeen gold beads
each one a flower
on a gold chain

I will give you
some bracelets
yellow snakes to coil
lovingly over your arms

I will hand you
my sharpest spear
that you may impale me
on our love

You are my wild
golden maned horse
I shall gallop you
miles into the night

ROULETTE

Destiny is
a tightening rope
swinging between
air and air

PSALM OF DEATH

Rejoice dearly beloved
we are gathered together
in the passage of time
to become jewels
wrought on a living scythe

THE GIFT

Speak now
of the golden horses
swifter
than the wind –
beautiful
the sound of their hooves
on
the ever changing ridge of light

Gold
captured in the light
of
changing winds –
uncontrollable
plunging of fierce breath
no hand
trembling can hold
such power